The Lemonade Mystery

Written by Jack Long
Illustrated by Leonard Shortall

Modern Publishing
A Division of Unisystems, Inc.
New York, New York 10022

TO AMANDA AND
STEPHEN - SHORTALL
L. S.

TO MY GRANDCHILD
NICHOLAS
C. D. L.

TO NINA AND JACK
RIESMAN
J. L.

Published by Modern Publishing,
a division of Unisystems, Inc.

Copyright © 1989 by Carlo DeLucia

TM—WHODUNITS? Mystery Storybooks is a trademark of Modern
Publishing, a division of Unisystems, Inc.

®—Honey Bear Books is a trademark of Honey Bear
Productions, Inc., and is registered in the U.S. Patent and
Trademark Office.

Printed in Belgium

TABLE OF CONTENTS

Chapter One . . . . Two Robberies 8

Chapter Two . . . . The Dark Cave 22

Chapter Three . . . . . . Another Robbery 36

Chapter Four . . . . Benny 46

Chapter One
Two Robberies

Brrnng! Brrnng!
Betty Beaver picked up the red phone in her detective agency.
"Hello. Betty speaking," she said.

"Betty, this is Rowdy Raccoon," said a familiar voice. "Can you come to my house at once? My lemonade stand has been robbed!"

Betty met her assistant, Perry Possum, on the way, and she told him what had happened.

"I was headed for Rowdy's anyway," said Perry. "The mayor asked me to deliver some letters for her , and one is addressed to Rowdy."

Rowdy met them at the gate.

"I'd just sold the last cup of this morning's batch of lemonade. I made one more jugful to donate to the mayor's annual picnic—and someone stole it while I wasn't looking!"

"That's right," said Perry. "The mayor's picnic is today!"

"Well, we have one clue already," Betty said. "Now we must look for others."

"Clues?" Rowdy was puzzled.

"Little bits of information that help us learn about the crime or who did it," said Betty. "The first clue was that the thief took something to drink. So we know that he was thirsty."

"Look at these big footprints!" said Perry.

"Clue number two," said Betty. "The thief has big feet. Let's follow his prints."

Betty, Perry, and Rowdy followed the trail
of footprints. Suddenly, Perry stopped.

"What's that noise?" he asked.
"I think it's someone crying," said Betty.

They found Flossie Raccoon crying by her window.

"What's the matter, Flossie?" Rowdy asked.

"The mayor asked me to bake her favorite cookies for the picnic today. I left them on the sill to cool, and someone took them!"

"Ah–ha!" said Perry. "First the lemonade and now some cookies are stolen."

"Clue number three," said Betty. "Now we know the big-footed, thirsty thief was hungry, too!"

They promised Flossie that they would look
for her cookies, as they said goodbye.

Chapter Two
The Dark Cave

They followed the footprints to a big cave.
"Come on," said Betty bravely. "We have
to go inside."

It was very dark inside the cave. Perry
Possum gave them each a lighted candle.
"Anyone here? . . . here?" her voice echoed.
There was no answer.

They were heading towards an opening in the far wall of the cave when they heard a very peculiar sound.

It was a fluttering sound.
It was a squeaky sound.
It came from overhead.
They all looked up.

25

On the ceiling were many small, bird-like creatures. Bats!

"Hello," said their leader. "May we help
you?"

"We're looking for a thief," said Betty.
"A thief who stole my jug of lemonade and some cookies," Rowdy added.

"We followed his footprints into this cave,"
said Perry.
Squeak! Squeak! All the bats started
speaking at once.

"Someone came through here before but
we didn't get a good look at him," they said.

"When he left, he hit his head on the opening," said the leader, "and cried *'Ouch!'* in a deep, growly voice."

"Clue number four," said Betty. "The thief
is tall."

"And he has a deep, growly voice," Perry
added. "Now we have five clues."

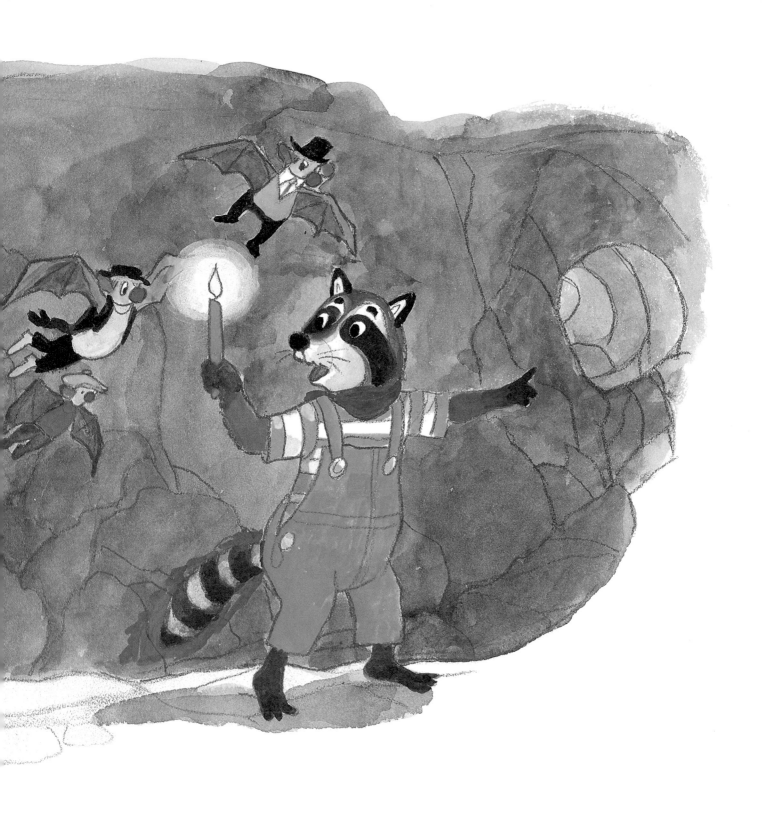

"This opening leads into a tunnel," said
Rowdy.
"Come on," said Betty. "Let's follow it!"

It was as dark as a moonless night in the
tunnel. They stumbled around a turn.

"Look!" cried Betty. They saw a light up ahead.

Chapter Three
Another Robbery

They headed for the light and soon walked
out of the tunnel and into a sunshiny meadow.
Perry pointed to the ground.
"Here are the footprints again," he said.
"Let's follow them."

The prints led them to a family of field mice,
who were running all around.

"What's wrong?" Betty asked.
"Someone stole the cheese we were going to bring to the mayor's picnic today!" said the father mouse.

CRACKERS

"Did you see the thief?" asked Perry.

"No," the mouse answered. "But we found some hairs of dark brown fur on the cheese storehouse floor."

"Clue number six," said Betty. "The thief has dark brown fur."

"I'm forming a picture of this thief in my mind," said Rowdy. "It was someone who was hungry and thirsty, has big feet, is tall, has a growly voice, dark brown fur … and I'm beginning to think he doesn't like mayors or picnics!"

"Let's find him," said Perry.

They followed the prints through the meadow.

Suddenly, Rowdy stopped. "Look!" he cried.

Just ahead, they saw a brown, furry hill. All at once, the hill stood up!

Chapter Four
Benny

"A bear!" cried Perry.

"Hello!" said the bear. "I'm Benny, and I've just moved to Good Forest. How do you do?"

At his feet lay the lemonade, cookies and cheese.

"Clue number seven," said Perry. "The thief is a big, brown bear named Benny!"

"Thief! Me?" said Benny. "I don't think that's a very nice thing to call a new neighbor."

"It wasn't very nice of you to steal the mice's cheese, or Flossie Raccoon's cookies, or my lemonade, either," said Rowdy.

49

"Why did you take those things?" asked Betty.

"The mayor asked me to help carry things to the picnic because I'm big and strong," said Benny. "She gave me a list of Good Foresters who would have supplies waiting for me."

"The mayor didn't tell me anything about that," said Rowdy.

"Maybe she tried to," said Betty, "but you
didn't get the message."

"Perry," Betty said, "didn't the mayor ask
you to deliver some letters this morning?"

"Oh no!" Perry said. "I forgot! That's why I went to Rowdy's this morning—to deliver this note!" He pulled an envelope out of his pocket.

Rowdy Raccoon

Rowdy opened the envelope.

"Sure enough!" he cried. "It's a message from the Mayor telling me my new neighbor, Benny the bear, would be by to carry my lemonade to the picnic!"

"I have one here for Flossie and the field mice family, too!" cried Perry. "I'm sorry I called you a thief, Benny. I feel so dumb!"

57

"There, there," said Benny, patting Perry's shoulder." That's okay. You just forgot—that's not being dumb."

"And you forgot because you were trying to help others," said Betty. "Let's put all this behind us and start getting to know our new neighbor!"

Betty, Perry, Rowdy and Benny had a nice, long chat and by the time everyone arrived for the picnic, they were becoming fast friends.

"I think you're a very smart detective," Benny said to Betty. "How did you ever figure this whole thing out?"

"It's easy," smiled Betty. "I just followed the 'bear' facts!"